# MASHA

## AND THE FIREBIRD

MARGARET BATESON HILL

ANNE WILSON

Earth and Water, Fire and Air,
Firebird's eggs so rich and rare.
Life and Death together dwell,
Cradled by love in a perfect shell.


Бережет Жар-Птица диковинные яйца –
Землю и воздух, и огонь и воду.
А внутри, чудесной скорлупою скрыты,
Почивают мирно жизнь и смерть, сплетясь.

O N THE EDGE of a deep, dark forest there once lived a young girl called Masha. Every day her father would go into the forest to chop wood while her mother would cook and sew. Masha herself looked after the hens, and every day she would go and collect their eggs in a little basket. Once a week Masha's family took the eggs and the bundles of wood to the nearby market town to be sold.

ONE DAY at the market Masha saw a tiny box of paints for sale and, because her mother had sold all the eggs she had brought, she bought the paintbox for Masha.

When they got home, her father suggested to Masha that she might like to paint some of the hens' eggs – why the Tsar himself had a collection, exquisitely decorated with gold and jewels!

MASHA LOVED to paint the smooth shells of the eggs and sometimes, while the paint was drying, she would run off to play in the forest.

MASHA KNEW the forest around her home well, but one day she ventured further than usual and found herself deep in the heart of the forest where the old trees grew and the air was dark and still. She sat down on a mossy stone and wondered which way to go. Suddenly, from high above her, she heard someone call her name.

MASHA LOOKED UP. In the gloom of the forest, a flash of brilliant feathers blazed out of the darkness, as fiery sparks of light fell cascading to the ground.

"Masha," said the Firebird, for that was who it was, "I need your help. I am the guardian of the eggs of the Four Elements. Baba Yaga is trying to steal them, and if she does she will gain all their power for herself."

"But how can I help you?" asked Masha.

The bird showed Masha its nest – four eggs lay nestled inside. "If you paint them, I can hide them from Baba Yaga."

MASHA TOOK the first egg, the egg of Earth, and wrapped it carefully in her handkerchief.

"But how will I find you again, I don't even know the way home," said Masha.

"This feather will guide you," said the Firebird, plucking a small feather from its wing.

Masha held up the feather and immediately it lit up a small path in front of her. Following this light she travelled home safely.

MASHA HURRIED into her bedroom and took out the egg of Earth. It was a pale, greeny white and smelt of the rich forest soil.

She started to paint the egg, covering its shell with mosses and lichen. Hidden amongst tiny leaves, small flowers began to bloom and mice and squirrels peeped from the roots of trees. Finally, in the centre of the egg, she painted a large grey wolf. She could almost hear him padding off into the forest.

FOLLOWING THE LIGHT from the feather, she took the egg back to the Firebird. Together they went to the very heart of the forest and the Firebird placed the egg deep in the hollow of a mossy bank.

Later that day, when Baba Yaga was out collecting mushrooms, she passed close to the egg of Earth, but she did not see it.

Бережет Жар-Птица диковинные яйца -
Землю и воздух, и огонь и воду.
А внутри, чудесной скорлупою скрыты,
Почивают мирно жизнь и смерть, сплетясь.

WHEN THE FIREBIRD saw that the plan had worked, it gave Masha the egg of Water. As Masha held it in her hands she could hear the sound of water rushing down falls and the low, soft murmur of a faraway sea.

This time, she painted the pale blue of streams and the deep azure of the oceans, and in these waters rainbow-coloured fish swam by pale, pink shells and tangled water weed.

ONCE AGAIN, following the light from the feather, she took the egg back to the Firebird. Together they went into the heart of the forest, and the Firebird placed the egg in a still, deep pool where it sank silently to the river bed.

Later that day, when Baba Yaga was out fishing for eels, she passed very close to the egg of Water, but, as before, she did not see it.

Бережет Жар-Птица диковинные яйца -
Землю и воздух, и огонь и воду.
А внутри, чудесной скорлупою скрыты,
Почивают мирно жизнь и смерть, сплетясь.

THE THIRD EGG was the egg of Air. It felt light and fragile and when Masha held it she felt a soft gentle breeze on her face.

On one side of the egg she painted a golden sun bursting through soft, white clouds, and in this sky a giant eagle hovered. On the other, she painted a still black night, lit by a silver moon and tiny sparkling stars.

ONCE AGAIN, the light from the feather led her back to the Firebird and together they went to the edge of the forest. The Firebird flew into the sky and placed the egg deep in the clouds.

Later that day, when Baba Yaga was flying in the sky collecting cobwebs, she passed very close to the egg of Air, but, as before, she did not see it.

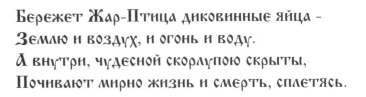

Бережет Жар-Птица диковинные яйца -
Землю и воздух, и огонь и воду.
А внутри, чудесной скорлупою скрыты,
Почивают мирно жизнь и смерть, сплетясь.

NOW ONLY THE egg of Fire remained. This was the most precious of all – the Firebird's own egg. As she held it in her hands, Masha could feel the warmth and love that flowed from its small white shell.

She mixed up paints of crimson and vermilion colours from the very heart of the fire. She painted glowing coals and leaping yellow tongues of flame, until the egg was ablaze with colour… and her paint box was empty.

MASHA HELD THE EGG. It was very beautiful, so beautiful she wanted to keep it for herself – why the Firebird had three eggs already! Then, suddenly, the egg became too hot for her to hold and she felt ashamed. She held out the feather and was just about to take the egg back, when her mother called to her: "Masha, be a good girl and take this basket of food to your father."

Бережет Жар-Птица диковинные яйца -
Землю и воздух, и огонь и воду.
А внутри, чудесной скорлупою скрыты,
Почивают мирно жизнь и смерть, сплетясь.

MASHA RAN all the way there and all the way back. Then she went straight to the table where she had left the egg — but the egg of Fire was gone!

Masha turned to her mother and asked in a trembling voice, "Mother, where's the painted egg that I left on the table?"

"While you were out, an old woman came to buy some eggs," said her mother, "she saw your egg and admired it so much that I gave it to her. You have so many, you won't miss one."

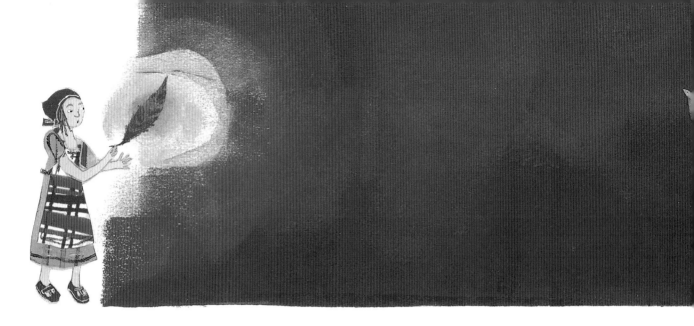

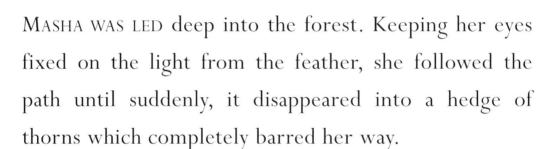

MASHA STARED in dismay – the old woman was Baba Yaga. She was very frightened, but she knew what she must do. She held up the Firebird's feather and said, "Show me the path that leads to the house of Baba Yaga."

MASHA WAS LED deep into the forest. Keeping her eyes fixed on the light from the feather, she followed the path until suddenly, it disappeared into a hedge of thorns which completely barred her way.

Masha tried to push her way through, but the needle-sharp thorns tore at her hands and arms.

Masha sobbed in despair, then she heard the soft padding of feet and a low voice said to her, "Climb on my back and I will leap over the hedge."

Masha turned to see a large grey wolf. She sat on his back and he leapt high over the hedge of thorns. Then he set Masha safely down, and disappeared back into the forest.

MASHA RAN on quickly, but then had to stop for a second time – a fast flowing river cut across her path. It was very deep and Masha could not swim.

"Hold onto my fin and I will swim you across the river," said a quiet voice from the water. Looking down into the water, Masha saw a rainbow-coloured fish rise to the surface.

THE FISH carried Masha safely to the far bank
and then it sank back down into the waters.

Masha ran on, but suddenly found herself lost in
a swirling mist. Which way should she go? Above her
came the sound of powerful wings beating the air and
an eagle lifted her high up into the air and out over the
mist. The eagle set Masha down by an old gate.

BEYOND THE GATE lay a house that was whirling and twirling around on a chicken leg. In front of the house stood Baba Yaga! The old witch was as big as a mountain. She had great thick arms with large thick hands, and her mouth... her mouth was a wide, dark cave and it was full of large, iron teeth.

Bravely, Masha pushed open the gate and slowly walked towards Baba Yaga, until the witch and the young girl stood face to face.

"Have you come to fetch the egg little girl?" sneered Baba Yaga, "here it is in this basket. Come and get it... if you can!" and she threw back her large ugly face and laughed, her iron teeth glaring from her wide mouth.

But Masha was still carrying the Firebird's feather in her hand, and holding it up high she called out, "Dear Firebird, Guardian of the eggs, come quickly to help me!"

FROM DEEP in the forest came a long answering cry and in a brilliant flash of light, the Firebird burst from the trees.

The laughter on Baba Yaga's lips died and she reached out with her powerful arms to catch the Firebird. The Firebird did not try to avoid her grasp and, as Baba Yaga's hands tightened around its neck, the Firebird became a blazing mass of flames.

Masha realised that this was her chance to rescue the egg. She ran to the basket and took the egg just as Baba Yaga threw the Firebird to the ground.

AS THE FIREBIRD lay burning in its own flames, it called out to Masha, "Throw the egg into my flames!"

So Masha threw the egg deep into the heart of the fire, and as she did, the blazing flames engulfed everything around her.

WHEN MASHA opened her eyes, night
had fallen. She was lying all alone in
the small clearing. Baba Yaga and her
house had vanished and there beside
her lay the cold, grey ashes of the
Firebird and its egg. Sorrow over-
whelmed the little girl and she lay on the
soft earth weeping until the tears would
come no more. At last, far above her, the
first rays of the morning sun awoke the
eastern sky. Then another light caught
Masha's eye.

A small flame sprang from the ashes. It was
followed by another. The fire grew hot and bright,
and then came the sound of an egg cracking open. In a
flurry of fire and feathers the Firebird was born anew
from the flames!

Masha laughed and clapped as the Firebird flew
round her head, its shimmering tail feathers brushing
her cheek. Finally, the Firebird flew away into the
morning sky, and at her feet Masha found a tiny box of
paints…

*Decorate your own eggs!*

The craft of decorated eggs is widely practised throughout Europe, especially at Easter. There are many different ways to do this: dying, painting or collage. Here are a few ideas to get you started.

*Prepare your egg:*

If you want to use a real egg, hard boil one in a pan for about 20 minutes. Then let it go completely cold before you start to decorate it.

If you make a papier-mâché egg, you can make it any size you want. Blow up a balloon to the size you want. Then, using a paint brush, stick torn strips of newspaper (3cm x 3cm/1.5in x 1.5in) onto the balloon with glue (a cold water paste or watered down PVA) until the whole balloon is covered.

Leave it to dry, then repeat until the balloon is covered with about five layers of paper. For the top layer use plain white paper, instead of newspaper.

*Now you can decorate your egg:*

Simple patterns are the easiest. Start by painting your egg one colour all over.

Then use a different colour to add spots, stripes or zig-zags. Felt tips are good if you want to do more complicated pictures. Or you could cover the egg

with tissue paper, pictures from magazines, stickers or even pieces of fabric and lace. Try to come up with some ideas of your own. The most important thing is to have fun!

THE POEM YOU CAN SEE IN THE BOOK is written in Russian using the Russian Cyrillic alphabet. This alphabet is based on the Greek alphabet and was invented by the Russian Saint Cyril, who used the letters to translate the Bible into Russian in the ninth century.

Five of the letters are exactly the same as English:
A, K, M, O and T.
Seven look like English but are pronounced differently:
B, E, H, P, C, Y and X.
There are 21 more letters giving a total of 33 — seven more than are used in English.

Бережет Жар-Птица диковинные яйца –
Землю и воздух, и огонь и воду.
А внутри, чудесной скорлупою скрыты,
Почивают мирно жизнь и смерть, сплетясь.

*For the Morris Family, M.B.H.*

*For all my smiling friends, A.W.*

Published by Zero to Ten Ltd.,
a division of the Evans Publishing Group
2A Portman Mansions
Chiltern St
London WIU 6NR

Reprinted 2005 (twice)

Original hardback edition published in 1999
Copyright © 1999 Zero to Ten Limited
Text copyright © 1999 Margaret Bateson-Hill
Illustrations copyright ©1999 Anne Wilson

First published in paperback in Great Britain in 2001

Russian text by Michael Sarni

Publisher: Anna McQuinn
Art Director: Tim Foster
Senior Editor: Simona Sideri
Publishing Assistant: Vikram Parashar

A CIP catalogue record for this book is available from the British Library.

ISBN 1-84089-201-3

Printed in China

Earth and Water, Fire and Air,
Firebird's eggs so rich and rare.
Life and Death together dwell,
Cradled by love in a perfect shell.

Бережет Жар-Птица диковинные яйца -
Землю и воздух, и огонь и воду.
А внутри, чудесной скорлупою скрыты,
Почивают мирно жизнь и смерть, сплетясь.

## Folktale Series

Drawing on traditional themes,
Margaret Bateson Hill has written four
beautiful new stories. Each time, the heroine
uses a local craft to solve her problems
and instructions are included at the back
so children can try it out themselves.

•

*Lao Lao of Dragon Mountain*
illustrated by Francesca Pelizzoli
with Manyee Wan and Sha Liu Qu
HB: 184089-047-9 • PB: 184089-046-0

Delicate artwork provides a perfect context
for this beautiful story set in China.
Featuring the full story text in Chinese
and paper-cutting instructions.

•

*Shota and the Star Quilt*
illustrated by Christine Fowler
with Gloria Runs Close to Lodge
HB: 184089-063-0 • PB: 184089-202-1

Stunning, naïve artwork beautifully
complements this moving story of
a modern Native American girl.
Featuring the full story in Lakota
and a fantastic collage project.

•

*Masha and the Firebird*
illustrated by Anne Wilson
with Michael Sarni
HB: 184089-134-3 • PB: 184089-201-3

Magical artwork enhances a poetic story
of a Russian peasant girl.
Featuring poetry in Russian
and an inspiring egg-painting project.

•

*Chanda and the Mirror of Moonlight*
illustrated by Karin Littlewood
with Asha Kathoria
HB: 184089-183-1

Exquisite watercolours capture
the atmosphere of Rajasthan in India.
Featuring the full story in Hindi,
and an engaging mirror-decorating project.

## *English four to eleven Award for the Best Children's Picture Books of 1999*

*Masha and the Firebird* is a delight
because, whilst it has resonances of other
traditional stories, it is an original.
The text is interwoven with images of
traditional tales and the brilliant
illustrations illuminate the story.
As the reader, you have shared in
the painting of the eggs and you are
then encouraged to decorate your own.
Imaginative and stimulating, the reader is
drawn back to read the story or feast
on the pictures. Wonderful!

•

MARGARET BATESON HILL was born
and grew up in Blackpool, Lancashire.
At University she studied Drama and English.
Now Margaret spends her days sharing stories
with children and adults in schools,
museums and libraries.

Margaret enjoys meeting people from different
cultures – this, she says, makes Brixton in South
East London the ideal place to live as it is
definitely one of the cross-roads of our world.

ANNE WILSON was born on the tiny Ascension
Island in the South Atlantic and grew up in
England. She travelled extensively in Africa
and South Africa and studied illustration at
Bath College, graduating in 1996.

The blending together of colour, collage
and print is a central feature of Anne's work
and details from her environment and the range of
places and cultures which she visited
come through in her images.

MICHAEL SARNI was born and grew up
in Kiev, in the Ukraine. He now lives and
works in London, where he makes computers
behave for a living! He remembers well going
with granny to market only to discover 1001
wonders the world is made of.

---

ZERO TO TEN books are available from all good bookstores.

If you have any problems obtaining any title, please contact the publishers:
ZERO TO TEN, 2A Portman Mansions, Chiltren St, London W1U 6NR Tel: 020 7487 0920